for Iris

The Umbrella

Lisa Lebedovich

SIMPLY
READ
BOOKS

There once was a boy named Sebastian who discovered
a little grey rain cloud floating above his head.

He did not know where it came from
or how it got there, but he did know
he did not like getting wet.

So he found a big umbrella
to carry just in case it rained.

He brought it to the park.

To take his dog for a walk,

and even to music class.

Everywhere Sebastian went,
the rain cloud went,
and so did his big umbrella.

The umbrella kept him safe and dry from the little cloud.
But it made it hard for Sebastian to play games,
and meet new friends.

Riding a bike was no longer fun.

Neither was watching his favourite show.

The upside was that he never had to share a seat on the bus.

But he had no one to talk to or trade sandwiches with.

Until one day, he was playing a game of kick the acorn,

They sat together for hours, looking up at the stars,
sharing stories and trading sandwiches.
Like new friends do.

Thanks to Alicia, Judith, Megan, Julie & Cole

Published in 2021 by Simply Read Books
www.simplyreadbooks.com

Text and Illustrations © 2021 Lisa Lebedovich

Library and Archives Canada Cataloguing in Publication
Title: The umbrella / Lisa Lebedovich.
Names: Lebedovich, Lisa, 1976- author, illustrator.
Identifiers: Canadiana 20200291394
ISBN 9781772290523 (hardcover)
ISBN 978-1-77229-069-1 (e-book)
Classification: LCC PS8623.E227 U43 2021 |
DDC jC813/.6—dc23

We gratefully acknowledge for their financial support of
our publishing programthe Canada Council for the Arts,
The BC Arts Council, and the Government ofCanada.

Manufactured in Korea
Book Design by Lisa Lebedovich and
Naomi MacDougall

10 9 8 7 6 5 4 3 2 1

Canada Council   Conseil des arts
for the Arts   du Canada

Canadä

BRITISH   BRITISH COLUMBIA
COLUMBIA   ARTS COUNCIL
                An agency of the Province of British Columbia